Rookery

Rookery Heights

Author Biography

Angela Craddock lives in the North East of England with her partner Anton and their fox terrier, Teddy. She greatly enjoys books, foreign travel and cooking as well as spending time with family and friends.

Her love of reading has been a lifelong passion along with a burning desire to be a writer. She founded The Buddies Book Club in 2013, bringing together a collection of friends who share a love of reading. All of those original members are still enthusiastic participants. She views reading as a way of broadening the mind; stories are gifts to us from authors who share observations from their unique perspectives. She finds writing to be a cathartic process of self-expression and an interesting forum that entertains her readers.

After working as a qualified nurse in the NHS for 35 years she has gained a wealth of experience and feels privileged to have helped her patients through every stage of life's bittersweet journey. She is educated to degree level having achieved a Bachelor of Arts degree and a Postgraduate Certificate.

Following her retirement in 2020 she is delighted to have written an extensive collection of short stories and a novella. Her best ideas spring to mind on breezy walks along the coastal path between Whitley Bay and Tynemouth.

She is living her best life and has stopped waiting for Friday!

Email: angelacraddock22@gmail.com

Twitter: @AngelaCraddoc12

Instagram: craddock.angela

Facebook: /angela.craddock.5

Occupation: Retired Critical Care Nurse and Infection Prevention Specialist.

Rookery Heights

Rookery Heights

This book is dedicated to my precious Mam Gladys Smith who is always the first to read everything I write. She supports me in all that I do and for that I am eternally thankful. Love always.

Rookery Heights

<u>Special Acknowledgements:</u>

To Anton for being my right hand man and my rock
and to Teddy for keeping me company while I write.

To Julie King, my dear cousin and dedicated reader of
my stories. Thanks for your unwavering interest and
enthusiasm.

To Lesley Beattie, my lovely friend. Thank you for your
positive feedback and for helping to build my
confidence as a writer.

To all the members of my Buddies Book Club: Patricia
Taws, Diane Rutledge, Lisa Wood, Sandra Sandy,
Stephanie Hannant, Judith Pike and Veronica Holland.
Thank you for supporting and encouraging me.

To Dawn Wilkinson, my new friend who has been
instrumental in this publishing process and leading me
forward. Thank you, I am hugely grateful and couldn't
have done it without your help and guidance.

Rookery Heights

<u>Contents</u>

Rookery Heights

A flickering candle,
A creak on the stair
Muffled cries in the dark,
You think no-one is there
Rustling in the hallway,
The doors mysteriously shut
Are you certain you're alone?
Can you really trust your gut?
Black eyes are watching you,
Spying from the rafters
Some are living but others have
Passed onto a life thereafter.

Rookery Heights

Rookery Heights

"Please listen to what I have to tell you. Rookery Heights is a place where bad, inexplicable things happen, a house on a hill with a history of darkness and bad omen. I strongly advise you not to go there, for I have experienced things I would not want others to see. You will notice an unkindness of ravens, sitting up on the high ledges and rafters in a row, like funeral directors, or swooping and diving, bat-like. The ravens will never leave because they are strongly entwined in the mysterious forces that surround the Heights. In many cultures the raven has connections with the underworld, with misfortune and death. Do you know the meaning of 'psychopomp'? Ravens are messengers that have the ability to transition between the material world and the spirit world; they escort newly deceased souls from Earth to the afterlife.

I know that you are already researching the history of the house and I understand your personal interest. There is certainly plenty of work for you there, with paintings that look onto the dimly lit corridors, the library, the parlour and drawing room. I know the Master is crying out for someone to restore his art collection and will pay handsomely. However, please take my word that fame and notoriety is worthless in the face of the possible misfortune that may ensue. Ultimately it is your decision, but I implore you to consider all aspects most carefully before entering into something that you may be unable to extricate yourself from…. Anon."

Chapter 1

Rookery Heights is a manor house with an enclosed yard, built in 1785. It belongs to the wealthy Charlesworth family, successful in the field of investment banking, they are lucky to enjoy the privileged lifestyles afforded to the rich in society. With its stark architecture, it presents as a building of foreboding. It stands at the top of a vast area of woodland which features a maze and ponds. It has an impressive gated entrance which can be seen from the end of a long winding avenue, gradually widening to reveal the house. Undressed limestone with a rubble filling forms the main construction material, a poorer alternative to the cut stone feature of many more grand houses built during this time. The decorative iconic porch, as featured in other such stately homes, contrasts with the relative simplicity of the rest of the building.

On entering the hall there is a double staircase that majestically sweeps down to the main hall. The ornate cast iron spindles fixed beneath the smooth wooden handrail make a dramatic statement. Curved walls bear many paintings of family ancestors glumly immortalised in oil on canvas. The tiled floor is an impressive work of art in itself, a tessellation of cream, grey and cobalt squares serves as an elegant and economical substitute for marbled flooring.

At the austere entrance to the servant quarters hangs a large, framed sign bearing a prayer for their protection. The ominous message reads,

"May heaven protect our home from flame,
or hurt or harm of various name,
And may no evil luck betide
to any who therein reside".

Bustling away in the scullery the maids are preparing dinner for Lord and Lady Charlesworth and guests. With so many to cater for, food preparation seems to be a continual cycle for the kitchen staff. On the menu this evening is Brown Windsor soup, galantine of turkey with home grown vegetables and treacle cake for pudding. Young Bessie is being scolded by Mrs Mathers the Cook, from whom she takes all of her orders, for unnecessary and excessive wastage. She has roughly prepared the potatoes by removing the peel in great chunks, which is not the required technique. The girl struggles with the simplest of tasks and appears to daydream of a life upstairs instead of applying herself to her chores. At times Bessie appears to be in a different world as she experiences momentary lapses of concentration. She suffers from *petit mal* seizures, a form of epilepsy which causes an interruption of ongoing activities and a vacant stare, though this has never been medically diagnosed. Mrs Mathers has difficulty in understanding if this is indeed a real affliction and affords her little sympathy. She suspects that Bessie may be a bit simple as she seems unable to apply herself to the most menial of tasks. Bessie becomes easily distracted and seems to tire in the face of her mundane yet demanding workload. The poor girl could do with a bit of kindness and compassion, but there is none. She has had a hard start in life; at 13 years old with only elementary schooling and poor family support, she has been forced into service in order to be spared from the workhouse. It was only a few weeks ago when she arrived and she is still crying herself to sleep every night. She has no mother and misses her elder sister but knows that her position here is a relative luxury compared to that of a Poorhouse pauper. Her days are long and arduous; her body aches when she falls into bed after working for seventeen hours, but she is thankful not to go hungry. Mopping the floors, polishing and scrubbing the cooking range and brasses are the chores within her remit, plus anything else as anyone sees fit.

Mrs Mathers seems particularly hot and bothered tonight and is looking forward to supping her daily beer allowance later, a special perk of her job. The responsibility of ensuring that her staff deliver the expected service sometimes weighs heavily and Miss Bessie is definitely not pulling her weight. She wipes the sweat from her temples and briefs everyone with their duties. No-one wants to get on the wrong side of Cook who has been known to brandish a rolling pin whilst chasing a feckless skivvy around her kitchen. She is slowed down by her general bulk and large swaying hips that barely squeeze through the gap between the range and food preparation table.

Chapter 2

At 05:30 Bessie is always first to open up the kitchen, a gloomy place at the best of times due to lack of daylight and dim lamps to illuminate the room. This morning she lets herself in and is surprised to see her exhaled breath hanging in the air. She has never found the room to be as cold as this and she feels a definite chill in the air. Her first task of the day is to stoke the fire and fill the huge boiling pot with water, then set it on the stove. This will raise the room temperature and at least help her to stop shivering. As she is filling the vessel she is puzzled to notice not one, but two smashed eggs on the floor. This is most strange as the eggs are stored carefully in the pantry with the door kept closed to dust, insects and vermin. Bessie began to clean up the runny mess, suddenly feeling fearful that Cook might think that she had broken the eggs, or worse still, had eaten them, as all food is strictly accounted for. The lamplight flickered, dimmed, flickered brighter again. From inside the pantry came laughter followed by the noise of something smashing onto the floor. Bessie's heart began racing as she made her way to the walk-in cupboard to investigate. She nervously tried turning the door knob this way, and that, but the handle did not budge and the door remained firmly locked. She kept trying until it eventually released. On entering she saw a large earthenware container lying broken, its flour contents spilled in a heap. The door immediately slammed shut with force and Bessie screamed, for there was no-one there, and no possibility of a through draught. The girl was terrified, knowing her screams would not be heard and that she was going to be in a lot of trouble over this. Cook already thinks she is a liability so this will be hard to dispel. What a terrible start to the day she thought miserably. She started sniffling and crying as she picked up the broken jar and went to collect the pan and brush to clear up the flour. Just then she felt something sharply jab her in the back and a voice from behind rasped in her ear, "Useless girl, I'm watching you, Bessie!" Shrieking, she ran from the kitchen, flinging herself on the stairs and sobbing and shaking uncontrollably.

The commotion was overheard by Sara, the housemaid, who was on her way downstairs. She sees that Bessie is distressed and sits down next to her to comfort and ascertain what had happened.

"Bessie, what's the matter, what's wrong? It's ok, I'm here now", she said comfortingly. "Bessie, speak to me, what is it?" she implores.

Bessie has stopped crying and is staring straight ahead, in a trance- like state. Sara slaps Bessie's cheek, her face is pallid and her eyes are wide and glassy. The stimulation does nothing to cause a reaction. Suddenly Bessie's leg starts jerking, the spasmodic movements spreading upwards to her arms which begin thrashing too. Her face has taken on a bluish tinge around her lips where frothy saliva bubbles form as her body convulses. "Help, help", shouts Sara as she heaves Bessie onto the floor with every ounce of strength she can muster. By now there are more staff on the scene, crowding around her, intrigued and repulsed at the sight. They are so engaged in the dramatic incident that they fail to notice the grey hooded figure that fades from sight as it transitions through the kitchen wall. Nor do they see the hovering ravens that are flying low to the ground, an omen of bad things to come.

Cook arrives and takes charge. She has heard that a spoon should be placed in the mouth to stop the tongue being swallowed, but Bessie's teeth are clenched tightly shut. She asks Sara, Mr Perkins the Butler and Charlie the Hall Boy to stop crowding around and to stand back. A few minutes elapsed. While she was thinking what to do next, Bessie stopped thrashing and lay quite still, breathing deeply now, as if sleeping. From under her skirt a wet puddle of urine seeps around her. Cook rolls up some tea cloths to put under Bessie's head. In a rare moment she performs a caring gesture. She strokes the child's brow and in a soft voice says, "It's ok, my love, you're going to be alright".

Addressing Mr Perkins she says, "Please tell the Master that Bessie has taken a turn and ask if Dr Gilesgate could kindly look in, when he is next in these parts?" As Bessie regains consciousness, Sara is tasked with changing her clothes and taking her back to bed. She asks Cook if a cup of hot rice milk could be spared, as it would surely bring Bessie some comfort.

"Now everyone, let's set to, and double quick. What a start to the day!" she exclaims. Only then does she see the eggshells and the broken crockery and she can't help cursing under her breath.

Chapter 3

Over a slightly delayed breakfast Lord and Lady Charlesworth discuss the incident in the servant quarters. Lady Charlesworth takes a strict line with her servants but also feels responsible for their welfare. She hasn't had much contact with Bessie in these first few weeks of her employment and is concerned that she is unwell. This is not the first time there has been a disturbance in the kitchen shortly after the arrival of a new scullery maid. In fact, it could be better described as a recognised pattern, or reccurence of unexplained breakages, misplaced items, doors slamming and whispered voices. The last time it happened, Lord Charlesworth discussed their problems with Father O'Leary, for he had heard that such things may be attributed to poltergeist activity. The priest did acknowledge that a spirit can feed on residual or negative energy associated with a living person or location. He has heard that a person-focused poltergeist can become attuned with a female adolescent who is suffering emotional turmoil. In this perfect storm their combined energies can create telekinesis, whereby objects move or can be destroyed by the living mind.

Lord Charlesworth tries to hide his concern from his wife. "Try not to worry about it, my dear," he reassures.

"The girl is ill and needs medical, not clerical help. I am going to ask Richard to examine her. He may give Bessie something from the apothecary, some potion that will help. We will do what we can to make her well. It's our moral duty."

They exchange knowing looks. "It's all starting up again and it frightens me. I fear for us all," replies his wife despairingly.

Alfred Fallowfield has a passion for books. As a very good friend of Lord Charlesworth he has been granted open access to the library at Rookery Heights. He is a portly chap, smartly dressed and meticulous in his appearance but for his waistcoat which strains at the seams. His other passion is for rich food sloshed down with copious quantities of Madeira dessert wine. Standing at the main door he rings the bell to announce his arrival, and is soon greeted by Sara.

"Good day Mr Fallowfield," says Sara, bobbing to one side to allow his entry. "Shall I tell the Master you are here?"

"Thank you, I'd be obliged if you would. I'll be in my usual spot in the library, if he wishes to see me. Otherwise I will just let myself out when my eyes tire!"

He begins his ascent of the stairs, striding at first then slowing down as he catches his breath. He is very much looking forward to making some new book selections and dedicating more energy to his favourite pastime. He is very grateful that Lord Charlesworth allows him to use the library following his own devastating loss. Five years ago a fire started in the library at his home, Crosby Hall, resulting in the loss of many precious and valuable volumes of books. He tried to save as many as he could but in doing so suffered burns to his arms and hands. He cannot account for how the fire started; it is a mystery that cannot be solved. The first he knew was of an explosive, crackling sound that came from the bookcase, an extreme hot spot was seemingly created. A fire investigator could not determine how or why the fire had started and remarked that it was a most unusual occurrence. Alfred has a theory that it was a case of spontaneous combustion as Charles Dickens described in *Bleak House*, but he keeps the idea to himself for fear of ridicule. His flesh is forever disfigured, tightly retracted over the bone and serves as a constant reminder of the terrible event. However, he was lucky to survive. The same could not be said of his beloved special edition books whose pages were so quickly reduced to piles of ash. Some were salvaged, thrown from the windows onto the path below, but the acrid smoke clogged his lungs and he had to get out. He has since become strangely obsessed with the idea that certain combinations of books should not be piled up together, or lie together on the same spot, as they did on that fateful day. Such is his superstition, he selects just one book at a time, carefully replacing it when finished. His irrational compulsion is based on an extreme fear that history may repeat itself.

Chapter 4

Following the unfortunate incident at Crosby Hall, Lord Charlesworth has imposed a house rule that the fire must not be lit in the Rookery Heights library. The chance of an errant spark with the potential to cause such destruction makes the luxury of a lit fire too risky. All of his servants have been briefed on his specific instructions. The room is usually warm enough; the dark panelling and wall to wall bookcases appear to have an insulating effect. Alfred takes off his outer coat and unfastens the too small waistcoat. His belly breaks free. His eyes scan left to right, picking out his first book choice, *Frankenstein or The Modern Prometheus* by Mary Shelley. Firstly he runs his fingers over the book title, appreciating its fine quality and gilt lettering. Flicking through the pages to the first chapter he starts to read the opening lines. Lord Charlesworth pops his head around the door. He has come for a catch-up with Alfred and although he is not in the habit of drinking in the afternoon, he knows that Alfred will join him in a tot of cognac.

"Hello, dear chap!" is his cheery greeting, for he and Alfred have known each other almost all of their lives and are firm friends. They have many happy memories of climbing trees, scrumping apples and searching for bird's nests in the glorious summer days of youth. Their parents were business associates and this meant that the boys met regularly. As an only child, Alfred has always felt close to his friend who he holds in high esteem.

"Good to see you, Edgar," he says, ejecting himself from the chair in order to promptly shake hands. "How are you and Beatrice? Keeping well, I hope?"

"Thank you, yes, we are alright, though I'm having a problem with my new servant who has been unwell. If that weren't bad enough, things have started going 'bump in the night' again, well more like 'thud in the kitchen' if you know what I mean? Father O'Leary thinks things will settle down again but Beatrice worries about our unwanted guests and I don't want to make too much of a fuss and upset them downstairs," he replies, his index finger pointing to the floor.

"Well as long as whatever it is stays *below stairs* and doesn't come bothering us, we should be alright," Alfred chuckles, trying to make light of something that is clearly an issue of concern. "Nice drop of cognac!" he exclaims, and in doing so changes the subject.

"Yes, I wondered if you would like to share an excellent deal I'm considering. A couple of cases for you, a couple for me and we split the discount?" suggests Edgar.

"It's a pleasant little tipple so do count me in," says Alfred as he takes a sip, then raising his glass he goes on, "To your good health! Mind you, I should be cutting back on the stuff, for the good of *my* health. Heart keeps racing along, from time to time and I get a bit of pain, probably just indigestion, or it could be anxiety. I do think I bring it on by worrying….you know of my disposition!"

Edgar is only too aware that the fire in Alfred's library has had a damaging psychological effect and his friend is becoming increasingly obsessive. "Is there anything I can help you with, Alfred?" he asks out of concern.

"Well, my friend, when I next come over to collect the cognac I have some paperwork for you to look over. We will discuss it then if you might have the time?"

"Yes, of course, consider it done," confirms Edgar. Then, noticing the book lying at Alfred's side he remarks, "Frankenstein? Good God, man, you certainly pick them!"

Chapter 5

The first Tuesday of the month is a pleasurable day for Lady Charlesworth as she invites her friends to take afternoon tea. Mrs Mathers has been briefed on today's menu. She has ordered thinly sliced, buttered bread with potted shrimp, fancy biscuits and cakes all to be served on her favourite china. There will be a choice of tea, coffee, lemonade and ices which will be served in the parlour. She has invited her high society friend, Lady Caroline Neville to join her, and is keen to hear the London gossip and of her latest shopping trip. Caroline accompanies her husband on some of his business trips to the capital. She travels into the city four times a year to buy the most fashionable clothes in accordance with seasonal change. Venturing to Swan and Edgar, a luxury West end fashion store established in 1812, she looks at the latest styles in gloves, bonnets, parasols and muffs worn by ladies in 1875. Pretty ribbon sashes and cashmere shawls are her passion and she owns a growing collection of attractive combs and tiaras.

The parlour is decorated in blue and gold with heavy drapes at the windows to prevent fading of the rugs and upholstery. It is a showcase for the family's wealth and good taste with an eclectic array of ornate furnishings, statuettes and fine art as well as mementos. In the corner sits a pianoforte which was bought for Lady Charlesworth; as a fairly accomplished player she sometimes provides after-dinner entertainment for her guests.

Lady Neville has arrived twenty minutes before her time of invitation, as is polite and customary. Tea is already laid out and Lady Charlesworth asks Sara to show her into the parlour.

"How lovely to see you, my dear," says Lady Charlsworth, jumping up to greet her friend. "Are you well?" she asks, then without allowing time for a reply, she continues, "Now you must tell me about the latest fashions and goings on!"

Lady Neville pulls from her handbag a gift for her friend. It is an ornate hair barrette. "I want you to have this hair accessory, it's made from a new substance called celluloid, have you heard of it? All of the ladies will be wearing it soon. Even the gents are wearing it on their collars and cuffs. I had such an exciting time and Hugh allowed me to charge lots of lovely things to his account", said Lady Neville. "Not only did I augment my autumn wardrobe but I also popped to Fortnum and Mason! They have such delicacies and an array of speciality teas, my dear, there were so many I could hardly choose! I just had to buy a delightful picnic basket with a selection of biscuits and cheeses, wonderful for these last days of Summer." She paused for breath before continuing, "In the fashion store I asked the assistant to lay everything out so I could touch the fabrics and take them to the light. It's so important to see the true colours, you know. I can assure you it was worth their while as the final bill was quite substantial. I bought two petticoats, one trimmed with lace and the other made of flannel, so much cosier in cooler weather, I find. I have stockings and a new stole also made of silk. My bonnet is also new", she added, smiling as she turned around to show off its side view.

Lady Charlesworth suddenly gasped in horror when she saw the decoration on the brim. The colour drained from her face. "No, no, you absolutely cannot wear that in here," she cried.

"What's wrong, what troubles you so much?"

"It's the feather....of the peacock, its markings represent the eye of the female demon that spies on your home and family, it is very bad luck indeed, the harbinger of misfortune, illness and unexplained death of children."

"Oh, don't be so superstitious, I totally disagree, my mother told me they bring good luck and prosperity. They stand instead for beauty and richness in life", Lady Neville retorted.

"No! It's the eye of Lilith! I know this for sure. My beautiful Clara brought a peacock feather to me just before ….the tragic accident…. The She Devil was responsible for the death of my precious child, now go, you must go. I cannot have it near me, get out of my house!" She collapsed down onto the sofa and the sobs kept on coming until she could cry no more.

Chapter 6

Lady Charlesworth cannot help but recall the devastating event that happened four years ago. She has tried so hard not to remember, but today it has resurfaced in an unexpected and brutal way, an assault on her memory. She will have to go back over it now, refreshing every detail even though it's so painful to do so. Clara was the only child of the Charlesworths and at the age of six she suddenly became unwell, lethargic and feverish. The child had only been in the confines of the nursery and gardens, not in contact with the outside world so it was strange that she had contracted an illness. There were no other children at Rookery Heights at that time and no one else became symptomatic despite its highly infectious nature. Small round spots appeared first on Clara's trunk then on her face and limbs. Lady Charlesworth was horrified as she thought it might be small pox which would surely carry with it a death sentence. The sickly, pathetic child was looked after by both her nurse and her mother. Nursemaid Agnes Williams had seen enough cases before to be quite certain that this was chickenpox, which gave some assurance.

Doctor Parsons was asked to examine Clara and he too confirmed that she had chickenpox. Lady Charlesworth was overjoyed that Clara would most likely improve in a few days. Nursemaid Agnes felt that it was important for Clara to take some fresh air as part of her recuperation so they often went for short walks in the gardens. Sometimes they saw the ravens pecking around on the ground, to scavenge on whatever food they could find. Clara was frightened of the ravens even though nothing tangibly bad had happened. She disliked their blackness and sensed that their non-blinking eyes were watching her. Their low throaty calls alarmed her and made her run away in fear. She was with Agnes the day she first saw the peacocks and was utterly enchanted by them; such beautiful majestic birds in stark contrast to the ravens. They would quietly wait and watch for the entrancing moment when the feathers were displayed in their full glory. Afterwards they would play in the maze where Clara grew accustomed to its twists and turns, running ahead of Agnes and cleverly navigating her way through.

On the fateful day that was to change everything, Clara presented her Mother with a peacock feather she had found that morning. She was hardly prepared for the shocking reaction it received. A scream went up, Lady Charlesworth told her to throw it out of the window and to never, ever bring such a feather into the house again. Poor Clara couldn't understand what she had done that was so wrong. She thought it would be a nice surprise and her Mother would enjoy wearing it in her hair. Bemused and upset, she went to sit quietly in the corner, as she was instructed to do when naughty.

Lady Charlesworth then felt sorry that she had reacted so strongly, after all, how was the child to know about such things as superstition and bad luck? It was better, in fact, that she did not know and that she should remain ignorant of such things. She called Clara to her and gave her a hug, saying she was sorry for screaming. They would get some fresh air, play in the maze and then they would have a treat, some ice-cream. That would help to make things better, she felt sure. They buttoned up their matching blue coats and set off for their walk in the grounds.

Chapter 7

The baccata maze was once an attractive feature within the grounds. Of circular design with a folly at its centre, it has vertical tall hedges that form the passage walls. Two thousand yew trees make the multicursal path, once carefully manicured, but now becoming unruly. The yew tree was perhaps an unfortunate choice in terms of superstition and tree folklore. Sacred to Hecate, guardian of the underworld, the yew is also thought to be a magical and ancient guardian of the landscape. The gardens were not as well kept as they once had been, since the sudden retirement of Mr Barnabus, responsible for their upkeep. The estate was far too large for one man to look after and no-one applied for the position when it was advertised last Autumn. Without the level of attention that is required to keep the garden in shape it would easily become overgrown, especially if nothing was cut back before Spring. It was quite a few months since Lady Charlesworth ventured down here, though Clara and Agnes made regular visits. Lady Charlesworth was dismayed to see that the topiary, once precisely cut and with defined edges, was misshapen. She couldn't remember when she was last here but it certainly didn't look like this. She wondered if her husband was aware that the shrubbery needed attention; with so many important things to attend to, she doubted it. She would raise the issue over dinner and see if they could try again to appoint someone.

Holding Clara's hand they entered the maze together. Clara was by now laughing and chatting, the feather incident apparently forgotten. She asks, "Mama, did you know you cannot really get lost in a maze? Agnes told me to touch the hedge with my hand nearest to it and keep that same hand touching all the way, as I walk."

"Well, we will surely not get ourselves lost today, now you have told me that!" replied Lady Charlesworth. At the entrance and certain points along the way were golden marigolds, spider-like witch hazel and large chrysanthemum. Whoever planted them may have had knowledge of floriography; a cryptic communication through the arrangement of flowers, or maybe they were randomly chosen. It is just as well that Lady Charlesworth has no idea that in combination they are talismans of spells, sorrow and death. A cool breeze whips up as they begin their journey through the maze. Clara is reminded not to run too far ahead as she happily skips along, pointing out the things of interest that she has noticed on her previous visits. Lady Charlesworth pushes back an unruly bramble to avoid it scratching her face. When they arrive at the centre they will visit the folly, a miniature castle with a flight of steps following the curve of the drum tower. It is thought that the building was created primarily for decoration; it has an element of fakery as the 360 degree look-out fortress has played no part in the defence of the estate. No-one knows what it was used for, or indeed if it had any use at all, standing merely as a whimsical feature around which the maze was later created. So they found themselves at dead ends, turning left then left again to get back on course and finally they neared the folly. From the top of the tower a hazy figure looked out, watching their progress. It would soon be time to implement the plan.

Chapter 8

Clara hesitated at the foot of the stairs, having been
warned each time by Agnes that she must hold back at
this point. When her Mother caught up they climbed
the crumbling steps together, anticipating the view from
the top. Ivy had woven its way across some of the
windows forming natural blinds of foliage. The place has
an inherent dampness even in warm weather.
Following the winding staircase around to the top they
finally catch their breath and look through the
stonework crenels and merlons at the green fields.
There were ponds surrounded by tree groves with all
the glorious colours of nature in abundance. Perched
right at the top of the hill stands Rookery Heights, its
dark shape presiding overall. A sharp gust of wind
picked up some dead foliage, whipping the leaves up
with centrifugal force. They tried to catch some of them
and watched as the rest were swept from the top of the
tower, spiralling downwards.

"I think we should head back now, it's turning cold and I
don't want you getting a chill," said Lady Charlesworth.
They carefully made their way down and she reinforced,
"Please don't run too far ahead".

Clara re-entered the maze and after a few twists and
turns was startled to hear laughter, high pitched and

child-like. A canvas ball landed at her feet, having been thrown over the top of the hedge wall. She picked it up and called, "Who is there?" More laughter could be heard, then, a voice said, "Follow me!" Around the next bend she saw a cloth doll on the end of a stick, a soldier wearing a blue and red uniform, as if jumping along the hedge top, reappearing at intervals.

"Clara, come back, I told you not to stray!" urged Lady Charlesworth.

"I'm just around the corner, you will see me in a minute, Mamma," Clara replied, but she was distracted, entranced by the doll and curious to meet the new playmate. Running now, trying to keep the doll in view, she has already forgotten her Mother's instruction. Now she could see a girl doll in a long green coat covering a purple frock, bobbing along. Who was there, she wondered; this had never happened before when she came here with Agnes.

"Clara, come back here, I can't see you. Clara, come back now, I order you!" Lady Charlesworth's voice sounds anxious. Unsure of which way to turn now, she hesitates. Suddenly, something black flaps in her face, and then again, a single raven swooping and attacking her. She screams and tries to shield her face, stumbling along now, she trips up as her foot is caught in a tangled vine. "Clara, help me, help!" she shouts, but it is in vain as Clara is running further away, keeping pace with the dolls as they dance along. "Who is there?" Clara asks again. "I want to play!" When she reaches the exit to the maze she sees a girl of her own age wearing a cream smocked dress. Her face is contorted and her hair hangs matted and wild. She is carrying the dolls, running along and urging, "Come with me, I will show you something". Clara is compelled to follow, not even thinking of her Mother or getting into trouble, or any of the rules instilled by Agnes. Running now in pursuit of the nameless girl with the toys, she must keep her in sight. A blue ribbon slips free from her silky plaited hair and catches on a bush.

Lady Charlesworth is distressed, crying and lost in the maze. Her ankle is sprained from the fall so she can only hobble a few paces. If she can just find her way out of here she thinks Clara will be waiting at the maze exit. Well, that is all the hope she has to cling to.

The strange girl waits for Clara to catch up, then laughing still, she runs ahead to an area of dense shrubbery. The trees are getting thicker now and she catches another glimpse of her, waiting then capriciously running ahead. Clara is mesmerised by her. She wants to know who she is, where she lives, how has she not seen her before? The ground which was soft and springy is becoming boggy under foot. The girl seems to have stopped and beckons her on. "Clara, over here!" she shouts, "Come to my treehouse".

Clara moves slower now as her feet begin to stick in the mud. Where are they headed? She wonders, as she presses on. The leaves turn slippery and muddy sludge flows over into her ankle boots. The girl has disappeared from sight. There is no treehouse. Just ahead lies a pool which is slimy with green algae, its smell is dank and fetid. Evil hangs in a shrouded mist over the marsh and Clara is frightened now. "Mamma, Mamma," she shouts, "Help, save me!" for she knew something dreadful was about to happen when she saw the ravens circling overhead. Two long skinny arms shot up from the putrid pond, covered in slime. Bony fingers clawed at her. She was pulled roughly by the feet, then, dragged down into the pool until she was totally submerged in the quagmire. Sinister laughter echoed all around the grove and the six ravens of death hung around to see the last breath from Clara's chest bubbling to the water's surface.

Chapter 9

At Rookery Heights, Lady Charlesworth and Clara's absence has been remarked upon. Agnes is concerned as they should have returned some time ago. Mrs Mathers also thought it strange as Clara's supper had not been touched. Dinner was almost ready to be served and there was no sign of Lady Charlesworth. She and Agnes began to feel that something was wrong as they would always return for mealtimes and certainly before the onset of dusk. There had been no special instructions discussed and they felt uneasy. Agnes knew they had headed off to the maze and decided that they should ask Lord Charlesworth if he knew of their whereabouts. Shortly after that it was decided that Mr Perkins and Charlie should saddle up the horses and launch a search, on Lord Charlesworth's orders. Both horses were jittery, their ears were flicking back and forth and they snorted excessively, seemingly reluctant to leave the stable. Eventually they made their way down the hill, the riders looking and listening for anything untoward. Approximately halfway between the maze and the main pathway a dishevelled figure limped into view, her skirt in tatters and her hair all tangled.

"Help me, help!" Lady Charlesworth implored.

"Is that you, m' lady?" Charlie shouted.

"Yes, it's me, thank goodness you have come", she gasps. "Have you seen Clara? She is lost. I lost her at the maze. I hurt my foot and... she disappeared. What can have happened to her? I despair, please, you must find her." She broke down in tears, relieved that help had arrived but feeling increasingly fearful for Clara's welfare.

"I will go on ahead to look for her," shouted Mr Perkins. "Charlie will take you home and then will re-join me".

"Thank you, thank you, please find her, find my child," she desperately begged. Mr Perkin's horse cantered away and his voice could be heard calling Clara's name into the darkness, becoming faint until only the sound of silence hung heavily. He knows the estate very well, having lived there almost all of his life but he is still disorientated by the landscape and hindered by lack of light. One clump of trees looked much like another. Charlie rides back down and takes up the search in the opposite direction but after a few fruitless hours with no positive leads they decide to resume at daybreak. With heavy hearts they return to the house and explain that Clara has not been found. There is always the hope that she is able to find her own way home, but for now they can only wait and hope.

Lady Charlesworth is distraught, in fact hysterical, and Dr Gilesgate has prescribed some laudanum to try to calm her crazed thoughts. He is well aware of its highly addictive properties but thinks that the opium will help her to get through the night. She willingly took the tincture to numb her anxiety, wanting to shut everything out and sink into oblivion. She prayed that soon they would tell her of Clara's safe return.

Chapter 10

At daybreak Lord Charlesworth joined the search party, knowing that with every passing hour it would be less likely they would find Clara alive. His heart aches at the prospect that something terrible has happened to his daughter. He doubts that good fortune will be on their side, given the history of occult forces and mysterious phenomena associated with their home. Never before did he think that such evil could infiltrate his family, but now he is not so sure.

Late in the morning Mr Perkins finds a blue ribbon, the only remnant, the only sign that Clara must have passed close by here. He dismounts and tethers his horse to a tree. On foot now he looks closely for any trace, disturbed leaves, anything that might lead him to Clara. He shouts her name over and over, sees a trail of small foot imprints, then lines in the mud as if something, or someone had been dragged along. Then ahead his eyes alighted upon a shape that was floating in a murky pool; when he saw the little blue coat his worst fears were realised. "Oh no, not Miss Clara," he gasped, then, grabbing hold of the face-down figure he pulled her from the water. Her lifeless body sagged and her arms flailed as he lifted her to him. Her face was grey and wrinkled like that of an old hag, the nose and mouth blue tinged. Frothy green secretions ran down the face. Mr Perkins knows she is now nothing but an empty shell and that her soul has long since departed this life. He cries not just for the loss of the child, but also for himself as he must find strength to break the devastating news to her parents.

Lord Charlesworth felt it his responsibility to inform his wife that Clara had been found, though in tragic circumstances. He thanked Mr Perkins for recovering his daughter, appreciating that the poor fellow was himself traumatised by the harrowing discovery. He is desolate and heartbroken when he imparts the news and is unable to console his wife. When Lady Charlesworth learned of Clara's death her screams reverberated through the corridors and rooms and every corner of the house. The whole household was reeling in shock and grief hung so thickly in the air that it was tangible. The days and nights rolled into one and Lady Charlesworth spoke to no-one, ate nothing, managing to exist only in a laudanum induced semi-comatose state. Curtains were drawn, clocks were stopped and mirrors were covered with crepe and black ribbon. Family photographs were turned face down to prevent the chance of being possessed by the spirit of the deceased.

It felt as though nothing would ever be the same again and Lady Charlesworth's grief was so acutely painful. Wracked with guilt and self-loathing she asked what kind of a mother could lose her child and be so reckless. No-one knew exactly what brought about Clara's demise and there would forever be more questions than answers.

The child's body was cleaned and re-dressed, nestled within an open white coffin and surrounded by flowers. In the drawing room a candle burned continuously and she was never left alone, right up to the funeral. Professional photographs were arranged, 'momento mori', so that a portrait likeness could later preserve her image. The household entered a period of deep mourning with even the servants wearing black armbands. Lord Charlesworth wore a black suit and a black cravatte. Lady Charlesworth dressed completely in black, symbolic of spiritual darkness, and she would maintain this attire for a full year of mourning. Her skin was so pale it appeared translucent against the black parramatta silk and her slim figure was now further diminished.

The funeral arrangements were discussed with Father O'Leary. The hearse would be a white carriage with glass sides decorated in silver and gold. It would be drawn by horses with white feather plumes. Clara would be buried in the churchyard, not the estate, for in life, she could not be kept safe there. A marble headstone with chiselled cherubs and weeping angels would guard her final resting place.

Lady Charlesworth dragged herself through that most terrible day, numbed with the sedative effects of opium and with no desire to keep on living.

Agnes left her employment at the end of the month. With no child to look after there was no longer a place for her there. Whilst she felt desperately sad for the loss of Clara she was thankful that no blame could be apportioned to her. It would be advantageous to get away from this oppressive place and make a new start, she thought. Whispers in corners, Clara's imaginary friend and the dark creeping shadows had been most unnerving to live with. Though she had never voiced her concerns, she suspected that others are aware of the untoward happenings and of eerie feelings that something is just not right.

Chapter 11

Jack Fortesque-Merritt is a portrait and landscape painter who also repairs and renovates pieces of art. The young chap is becoming well known and revered in art circles. Today he is walking up the long drive to Rookery Heights to discuss a commission with Lord Charlesworth. Smartly dressed and walking with a spring in his step he feels optimistic of striking a lucrative deal. There is only one thing that he finds unsettling, and that is the anonymous letter that he recently received in the post, warning him away from Rookery Heights. Could it be from a fellow artist who is in competition for the contract, trying to frighten him off, or is it a genuine attempt to protect him? There certainly are a lot of ravens here, he notices, but the birds don't make him feel particularly uneasy, even as they flap and flock above him. Coming towards him on the path is a small hunched figure, clearly an older person with wobbling gait. As they are about to pass one another, Jack tips his hat and exuberantly says, "Good day to you".

Even beneath the veil he can see the wizened face which scowls at him and replies, "Keep away, young man. Heed my warning or you will be sorry!" Whilst the unfriendly encounter takes him aback, he performs an elaborate gesture, a sweeping bow, and replies with slight sarcasm, "Well thank you kindly," and passes her by. After a few paces he glances back and sees the figure continuing on her way. What he does not observe is that she fades from sight and just a few moments later becomes evanescent. Jack is undeterred by the hostile old woman and with a quickened pace he approaches the grand porch entrance of Rookery Heights. He is confident that he has the knowledge and ability required and is more determined than ever to seal the deal. Emma the maid opens the huge front door in answer to the bell and smiles at the handsome young man who introduces himself to her and explains the purpose of his visit.

He is shown into the hall and notices some of the portraits lining the walls just prior to his introduction to Lord Charlesworth. They go into the parlour to talk about the job requirements and the skills that Jack has to offer. Lord Charlesworth explains that some of the portraits are deteriorating over time and, he suspects, with exposure to light and humidity. He would like the restorative process to brighten up areas of discolouration so that his ancestor's images can be preserved for years to come. Jack explains that oil paintings can suffer expansion and contraction which causes wood and fabric to absorb moisture. This in turn can cause the paint to shrink and crack and the flaking paint begins to lose lustre. As they are discussing the paintings Jack notices small heaps of wood dust on the floor and points out that this may be evidence of infestation from woodworm, termites or silverfish. If this is so, urgent attention may be required to arrest further degradation. He would be happy to take a closer look and advise on the matter, and his services would initially be free of charge. He would then produce estimates for the restorative work and then Lord Charlesworth could decide if he would like to proceed.

Lord Charlesworth is impressed by the observant, articulate young man. He is concerned that urgent action may be needed to save the portraits and is soon shaking Jack's hand. He then asks if Jack might be interested in painting a portrait of his daughter from a photograph.

Jack hides his excitement at the prospect as he feels drawn to this fascinating house and its historic artefacts. He assures Lord Charlesworth that he will be able to produce a painting to his satisfaction as his attention to detail is second to none. He has painted military and historic scenes, portraits of nobility and he is ready to paint something really exquisite for this commission.

That evening, over dinner, Lord Charlesworth discusses the meeting with his wife, explaining that Mr Fortesque-Merritt is going to do some restorative work on the old portraits. He hesitates before admitting that the fellow has been commissioned to paint a portrait of Clara, for he is unsure of her reaction. They seldom even mention Clara's name, so sensitive are they that it will cause upset. They both know that her death is a wound which will never heal, that nothing can bring their daughter back and that is as harsh a reality as it was four years ago. He is surprised that she seems pleased and asks how long it might take and in which room it would look best. He wonders if a small amount of healing has taken place and is pleased that the conversation was cordial. It would be his last intention to hurt her any more than she is already hurt.

Chapter 12

It was agreed that Jack would soon start work. He is assigned a room where the natural daylight is optimum and he will transport his easels, paints and cleaning solutions to this new base. He has the option of living in, if he wishes, to save time travelling to and fro. Lord Charlesworth gives him free licence to decide, explaining that his friend, Alfred is a regular visitor to his library, coming and going as he pleases. The portraits requiring attention are identified and Jack's payment fee agreed. Jack cannot wait to start and is full of enthusiasm for the projects, and naturally, the prospect of financial remuneration. This commission will nicely add to his work portfolio and he hopes will attract more work of a similar calibre.

The renovation process starts and Jack is pleased that the first portrait cleans easily and the work is not as time consuming as he anticipated. The portraits that have holes in their frames are set aside so he can carefully investigate the problem and hopefully avoid any spread of infestation to the others. He looks through the collection and sorts them into categories, deciding on the order in which he will work on them. He remembers the photograph of Lord Charlesworth's daughter and removes it from the protective wallet. He looks at the pretty child who lies in repose, clutching a doll. There is something about her face that is a little odd, he thinks, but decides that it's due to the colouring technique. He wonders if he will meet her and find out the true colour of her eyes. He will produce a better quality portrait if he learns of her personality and manages to replicate it within his work. Before he starts painting her there is work that he must urgently attend to. He starts the cleaning process of the next picture, carefully working over its surface inch by inch. The work is absorbing and it pleases him greatly to see the dull colours becoming bright again, as they were when first painted by the artist. He would show his father that money can be made in the art world and this project will be a successful one. He wonders where he can wash his hands as it is important not to transfer sweat or grease onto the canvas. He leaves the room and whilst not wishing to snoop, he pushes the doors that are ajar and peeps in, trying to find the water closet. One of the rooms was grand, a dining room, then there was the library. The door to the next room was closed so he tried the handle and realised this was the nursery, it must be the little girl's room he reasoned. It was immaculate, with everything neatly and tidily in place. The bed was turned back, ready for this evening, and a small pile of folded clothes had already been selected for tomorrow. There was a large, exquisitely made doll's house and a baby doll in a pram, waiting to go for a ride. Just as he was about to move on he heard a creaking noise coming from the rocking horse in the corner, its head briefly dipped forward, then back, or at least he thought it did. Making his way to the next room, he found the W.C. that he set out to look for. He began washing his hands at the sink when the tap suddenly spurted out boiling hot water. It made him shout out and then he had to run the cold tap for a few minutes to cool down the scald. Glancing in the mirror as he was leaving, he felt that someone was standing behind him, an older man, at a glance. Peering close up at the mirror now he got a terrible fright, as it was his own face reflected there, though greatly aged. His eyebrows were grey and his eyes were hooded below the deep frown lines. He fled in panic, maybe it was a trick of the light, or a trick of his imagination. Whatever it was, he didn't know, but it disturbed him and left him feeling most uneasy.

Chapter 13

Lady Charlesworth is putting the finishing touches to her dress attire in preparation for dinner. It is ten years since she and Lord Charlesworth married so they are having a special anniversary meal this evening. Mrs Mathers has agreed to make chowder soup with fresh rolls, roast pork and vegetables followed by chocolate crepes. There was a decanter of port and a fine champagne that would be served on ice, in celebration of the occasion. Tonight is special for another reason, for Lady Charlesworth has been keeping a secret which she is about to share. For the last few weeks she has been feeling excessively tired and nauseous. It has been quite some time since she reduced the dosage of laudanum which she took freely every day, so it has nothing to do with those side effects. She still has a need for it but only occasionally and is pleased that she seems in control of her addiction. Now she has something to look forward to and is ready to announce that she is pregnant. A new baby will bring them joy once more. Clara can never be replaced but another child to love and care for will give her a purpose again. She is excited, delighted, and looking forward to the fuss and attention that she will be hers once again. She looks in her jewellery box for a special item that she wants to wear tonight. It is a small cutting of Clara's hair that is woven and sealed in a keepsake locket. She has not felt able to wear it until now. As she fastens it around her neck she notices the barrette hair clip that Lady Caroline gave her. She feels dreadfully sad about ordering her to leave and cringes in remembrance of that day. She hasn't seen her since and misses her lively chatter and friendship. She will wear the barrette too, and in a few days will write to her, to apologise for overreacting and ask her forgiveness. She hopes that Lady Caroline will also be excited at the news of her pregnancy.

The hair decoration is a lovely piece. She feels guilty for not looking at it properly and appreciating the sentiment of the gift. She fastens it at the side of her French pleat and admires herself in the mirror. It is a perfect finishing touch to her ensemble.

Husband and wife gently embrace each other and kiss, then take their seats in the dining room. She sits at the end of the table near the fireplace, as she always feels cold. Lord Charlesworth is happier at the far end of the table where it is cooler. The first course is served and they chat happily, reminiscing about their wedding day, trying their hardest to keep the conversation pleasant and uplifting. Neither one will touch on how their joy turned to sadness when a child they loved was taken from them. They talk about the estate and work in progress, issues among the staff and a proposed trip to the seaside. The champagne is poured and Lord Charlesworth stands up in readiness to give a toast. "My dearest Beatrice, thank you for our ten years together. I love you and hope we will continue to go from strength to strength. Wishing us health, wealth and happiness. Here's to us!" Lady Charlesworth clinks her glass against his.

"Darling, I have something really special that I have been waiting to tell you. I haven't had it properly confirmed...but I've been feeling very sickly lately...and have every reason to believe that..."

Lord Charlesworth is hanging on her every word and trying to anticipate what she is about to disclose when he thinks he sees a wisp of smoke rising from her head. He is so puzzled that he cannot verbalise anything and watches as more smoke curls and rises up.

"Dearest Edgar, I think I'm expecting our baby!" Suddenly a flame sparks and ignites in her hair, the barrette has spontaneously burst into flames. Her hair is melting around it and she can feel it burning her scalp now. Lord Charlesworth rushes over and pours a jug of water right over her head. "My God, you were on fire! Are you alright? How on earth could such a thing happen?"

And it seemed that just when things were getting better, that really was not the case.

Chapter 14

Alfred is back in the library and is nearing the end of Mary Shelley's Frankenstein. He has found it an inspiring, thought provoking read. The monster is portrayed as being afraid of fire, a dangerous source used for sustenance. Though it is a symbol of discovery and enlightenment, fire frightens him due to its deceptive qualities.

'*The cottage was quickly enveloped by the flames which clung to it and licked it with their forked and destroying tongues*'. Alfred considers this theme of pyrophobia, as it is something that badly affects him. Even small, controlled fires, lit candles, bonfires that could pose a threat to his personal safety can cause him anxiety. He worries about the potential of being exposed to his nemesis once again and how he might react. The mere thought of it stresses him, increases his heart rate and makes him tremble. The monster's first experience excites him, in as much as fire creates light in the darkness but also that it harms when touched. He learns that the natural world is a place of dark secrets, hidden passages and unknown mechanisms. Alfred ruminates on the supernatural elements of the book. He worries that too much knowledge and innovation may lead to connections with the dark side. It is most worrying, as is his phobia weighed against his obsession, which he finds difficult to balance.

His next book selection is the currently rather popular *'Jane Eyre' by Charlotte Bronte*. Thornfield Hall interests him not only because of its Gothic gloominess, empty rooms and unexplained happenings, but that it features a house fire which he finds terrifying though fascinating in equal measures. Jane associates her images of fire with brightness and warmth until a frightening incident occurs. As Alfred progresses through the plot he reads in chapter fifteen how Jane sees smoke in the hallway which billows from Mr Rochester's room. His bed and curtains are on fire so she throws water on them. Rochester tells her that the fire was started by a drunken servant but it was really started by his insane wife, Bertha. Alfred feels happier that it was not the servant who was to blame. This is a risk that he considers, that an employee might have issues and could cause a fire, by way of retribution. He sees this as a worse threat than a mad woman in the attic, for he lives alone at Crosby Hall and knows there is no such person there to fear.

Jack removes the backing board from the next portrait that he is going to restore and is shocked at the damage he has unearthed. It appears that the picture is being eaten away by *Anobium punctatum,* or woodworm, which have tunnelled extensively and reduced parts of the frame to sawdust. There are lots of small, round holes with fine powdery dust around them. He has seen a few times before and is now anticipating that this is not a random finding. He begins to catalogue each portrait with an added description of any damage he identifies. He is concerned that the restoration will be made more arduous by this discovery and he must exercise great care to ensure there is no spread of infestation to the rest of the collection. The damage seems to be confined only to the frame at present. He begins the cleaning process, starting at the outside and working inwards to the image of Lady Isabella Bartholmew. He brightens her face with a spirit based substance, touching up the colours of her complexion and clothing, then re-varnishes. It is very slow though satisfying work and Jack becomes wholly absorbed. Lord Charlesworth will be pleased to see his descendant looking so fine and rejuvenated, he thinks. As he works he is faintly aware of light footsteps running along the hallway. A door slams shut, he hears laughter, then a voice shouts, "Get out!" He jumps up, looking out to see who is there, but there is nothing, no-one. A small rag doll that has been left outside the drawing room door is the only notable thing. He returns to the portrait and busies himself again. After a few minutes there is more noise; this time it sounds like furniture being dragged along a wooden floor and the same door as before bangs shut repeatedly. Jack shivers as he becomes aware that the room temperature has suddenly turned very cold. Whilst he tries to work out why this is happening he notices an image moving in the gilt mirror above the fireplace. He moves towards it to investigate then hears a tap, tapping sound on the window, like a large branch striking the glass. Turning quickly to look over his shoulder he sees a grey shape outside of the window, peering at him, and the tapping noise continues. Jack is confused and wonders if the shape outside was that of the reflection in the mirror. He looks in the mirror and sees the same ghastly face as before looking back at him, the old man, a glimpse of his future self. Now he is shaken as none of this has an explanation. When the mirror drops off the wall and smashes onto the hearth he flees from the room, and the voice again shouts, "Get out, get out!" He needs to splash his face with cold water and to pull himself together. He is afraid but has no intention of discussing this with Lord Charlesworth, or anyone else for that matter. They will think badly of him, that he is a fool, or they may even question his integrity, or indeed his sanity. He decides to sit in the library while he gathers his thoughts. He realises this commission is going to be far more challenging than it first seemed, but he will see it through, no matter what it takes. He has his reputation to think of and he refuses to be intimidated. Perhaps he is over tired, he considers. He will have an early night and will be refreshed and revitalised for tomorrow's schedule of work. With no desire to spend the night in this place he makes his way downstairs. As he is leaving he is happy to see Emma who is always friendly towards him. He has noticed on previous occasions how easily she blushes which he finds mildly amusing. Today though she takes one look at him and with an expression full of concern she politely says, "Might I ask you if you are alright, Sir, you look as if you've seen a ghost?"

Chapter 15

When Jack returns the next morning he is not at all prepared for what he sees. He enters the drawing room and is met by a cloud of flying black beetles that encircle him, landing in his hair and sticking to his lips. He beats them off and rushes to open the window. Hundreds of them have formed a soot-like layer on the window which looks like a living blackout curtain, and they cover the easel. If they have become embedded in the canvas he will be devastated, even though he is neither responsible nor at fault. This is an unfortunate set-back, but he will clean up all of the bugs and thoroughly check the condition of the other art pieces. He starts by brushing himself down, and even when he is clear of them all he still feels itchy and traumatised by the attack. Where had they come from? He cannot understand it as the window was definitely closed and it's not as if they have just come out of the woodwork. It would also seem that no one had been in the room as they would have cleared away the smashed mirror shards, lying just as they were. He really must let the housekeeper know; he certainly hopes she won't think it was he who caused the breakage. Some strange things certainly happen in this house, he muses.

Eventually the room is cleared of all visible insect activity; he is back on tracks with his work and feeling positive again. He is looking forward to painting the child in the photograph and will replicate the photograph to his greatest ability.

"Ahh, there it is," Alfred mutters under his breath. He has been scanning along the bookshelves in search of *"The Picture of Dorian Gray' by Oscar Wilde* which irritatingly had not been filed correctly. The Gothic and philosophical novel, considered indecent, had been censored in support of public morality. Dorian Gray is the handsome subject of a full-length oil portrait, who sells his soul to the devil in pursuit of eternal youth and beauty. His image is captured in the enchanted painting that keeps him from ageing. With every sin he commits his portrait becomes tainted though he remains young and handsome. The story tells of how his shallowness and vanity leads to moral disintegration and eventual downfall. "He grew more and more enamoured of his own beauty, more and more interested in the corruption of his own soul." Alfred was keen to explore the evolving themes of the novel, such as murder, destruction of the portrait and a fire in the attic caused by a smashed oil lamp. He thinks about the similar themes in the three books he has chosen, he draws comparisons of the characters and the plot, and how fire features in them all. He does not know what he will do with the information for it has no use or purpose other than to fuel his interest and imagination. What he does know, based on his superstitious beliefs, is that the books must not lie together on the table at the same time, for goodness knows what might happen, and he does not need or want to find out.

Chapter 16

Victor Perkins the Butler has a long history and extensive knowledge of Rookery Heights as his father, Arthur Perkins served as Head Butler before him. He was a loyal member of staff who dedicated forty years of service to the Welford family who once resided here. The house has always been associated with mysterious incidents and has had more than its fair share of bad luck over the last century. In the kitchen, the servants often discuss things that they have observed. Sometimes they hear furniture being moved around, whispering voices and rustling skirts and they never discover where the noises come from. A newly positioned stack of tins was found on the bench by Mrs Mathers when she was the only one in the room. There was knocking on the window and sounds of something clattering down the stairs into the servants' quarter. There are too many occurrences without a good explanation.

Bessie has settled in much better by now and her and Sara are good friends. Bessie's condition has improved since she has taken regular medication; Calomel powders seemed to be successful in keeping her epilepsy at bay but its efficacy was short lived. Dr Gilesgate felt that laudanum may be the preferred substance so Bessie unwittingly takes regular doses of the 'air dried poppy' potion instead. It is known to be far more potent than the powders. When she told Emma that she had heard voices, Emma reassured her it was a side effect of the medication but Bessie thinks differently. She doesn't know whether to mention that she saw a servant who she had never met falling on the stairs, or heard the screams when her hand got forced into the mangle. Bessie's stories are always dismissed out of hand, with Mrs Mather's describing her as a 'fanciful' child with an overactive imagination. The others have also told her on many occasions that she is hallucinating as a side effect of her medication. She has heard this so often that she is beginning to believe it. Victor believes her accounts are true but doesn't think it would be in Bessie's best interests to hear this. Arthur had told him that a servant fell down those steep stairs just behind them and tragically broke her neck. He has seen for himself that the accident was documented in detail in the Rookery Heights diary ledger of the year 1819.

Another of the stories that he passed down to Victor was of a strange happening which involved William Welford, a previous owner of the house. He went away on a business trip and was staying in nearby Castle Cleugh for a few nights when he became a victim of a fatal accident. At dinner he had the grave misfortune to choke on a piece of venison. The meat blocked his airway and, at seventy six years of age, his life came to an abrupt end. On the day that he died, a chambermaid at Rookery Heights was cleaning his bedroom and turning his bed back. As she looked out of the window she said, "The Master has returned". She saw that William was on foot which was most unusual as he always travelled by coach. At the time she saw him he had already been dead for several hours. When his body was returned to Rookery Heights the coach and horses that carried it refused to enter the main gates, and a second team of horses would not enter either. This resulted in the staff having to carry his body up the very long avenue to the place where he rested until the day of his funeral. Several months later there were sightings of him, making an alleged ghostly appearance in one of the upstairs rooms. It seemed that 'The Man in the Mirror' did not want to leave his residence and would reappear when least expected, his presence could still be felt by an unfortunate few.

Arthur warned Victor to keep his wits about him at all times. He believed that it was possible to live at Rookery Heights without coming to any harm but that one must exercise caution and be prepared to see and experience mysterious things. He believed that the malevolent forces would never leave, therefore it was pertinent to try to live with them, and around them. The ravens could actually offer some protection from evil and their patterns of behaviour may give warning of something untoward in the offing. These birds mate for life, and each mated pair will defend a territory. They have coexisted with humans for thousands of years and have been revered as a spiritual symbol in folklore, which should therefore be respected and protected. Ravens can mimic sounds from their environment, including human speech and are capable of social interaction calls to warn of alarm, chase and flight. He remembers Arthur's cautionary words.

No personal harm has ever come to Victor, though he remains psychologically and emotionally scarred by the death of Miss Clara. The memory of recovering her little body forever fills him with a terrible sadness and whilst he tries to shut out the image, it returns to haunt him in his nightmares. It was no coincidence that Victor was the one to find Miss Clara. That particular marshy pond was just one of a few on the estate that was associated with a sinister past.

He recalls a similar tragedy which occurred many years before, in a place which later became known as the suicide pool. A young servant was dismissed from employment for becoming pregnant out of wedlock.

With no means to support herself she was distraught. In a desperate state she fled from the house and ran deep into the woods, happening upon a pool of black, dead vegetation in a spot where the sun could never shine. It was said that an evil spirit called out to her, goading and taunting her until she threw herself in and was drowned in the murky depths. Some of the stories he chooses to share, and some he decides are better kept to himself.

Chapter 17

After the disturbing setback caused by the insect swarm, Jack is progressing well with his cleaning and restoration. Today he is going to begin work on his portrait of Clara so he places the photograph at the top of the easel and selects the canvas he thinks will be most suitable. It is extremely important to him to get this right. He stares at the photograph in the light. How can he best capture the essence of this little girl, he wonders. If he could meet her, even briefly, that would surely help to inspire him. He thinks it strange that he has not seen her and decides that the nursery on this corridor must not be her room after all. He notices that she is very pale skinned and he cannot determine her eye colour. The eyes look as if they have been painted onto the photograph. He makes an assumption that she has blue eyes, which would surely go most attractively with her blonde hair. He starts by sketching an outline and is concentrating deeply, breathing slowly. He is totally absorbed in his work. After a while he stretches and walks around the room, considering how the drawing looks from different angles. Just before he sits back down he rubs his eyes. Globes of free floating lights have entered the room in different sizes and colours. He thinks it may be dust particles captured in the rays of a prism, but how can that be? The globular orbs swirl above and around the easel. Jack is transfixed and tries to work out what is happening. The door silently opens in increments and a young girl stands behind him, watching. He suddenly senses someone, something is there and jumps back when he sees her behind him. "Ohh, hello!" he gasps, clasping his hand over his heart. "My, you gave me such a fright!" His mouth was so dry he could hardly speak.

"What are you doing in my house Jack?" asked the child accusingly.

"Err...um.. I've been hired to work on some paintings". His hand gestures towards them. He politely reaches out to her but she stares blankly and his handshake is declined.

"I'm not used to strangers here, I don't like them. There is another man who comes here. I watch him from my corner in the library. He is fat and he talks to himself. He reads the strangest books and I know of his fears and phobias. I don't like him one little bit", she said flatly emphasising each word.

Jack stifles a strange gurgling sound in his throat. "Might, I guess? Are you called Clara? You look to be of her age?"

"I may be", she said. "Or I might not be". Her face was expressionless, her voice monotone.

"Well, are you, or aren't you?" asks Jack, now playing her at her own game.

"I used to visit here whilst I was looking for somewhere to....stay. I liked to torment Clara and tell her to do bad things but she wouldn't listen to me. I tried to get her into trouble. I drained her of energy and I even made her ill, but she recovered. I pulled her hair and broke her toys, and one day, when I decided I'd truly had enough of her, I led her away to a dark place. I made sure she didn't come back because I prefer it here on my own. My name is Briar. Would you name someone after a thorny shrub, Jack? Or would you give them the name of Clara, which means 'clear and bright', though she was not when I was finished with her. Her eyes were green, the same colour as the filthy pond where I had her drowned. She was dead when they took that photograph, you must have guessed. And I agree, Jack, her eyes do look strange! I will be here, watching as you paint and I will tell you if I approve....or not".

Chapter 18

Alfred has returned to the library after a week-long break. He is ready to make some more literary choices and thinks his next piece of reading might be *The Diary of Samuel Pepys.* He feels quite sure that this book will be in Lord Charlesworth's collection and his first thoughts are to seek it out. He loves books so much and sometimes feels real sorrow that there is so much to read and yet so little time. He heads straight to the back shelves in pursuit of the historic chronicle of London events, whistling in pleasurable anticipation of finding it. Sure enough, he locates the book and has a quick flick through the pages before he settles down to read it. As he approaches the easy chair, his favourite place to settle, he notices a lit fire in the hearth, something which is strictly forbidden, and that three books are piled up on the table. The hairs instantly stand up on the back of his neck. He knows that he always puts the books carefully away, so someone else has selected them and positioned them on the table. Sweat beads break out on this brow as he checks the covers. Frankenstein on the bottom, Jane Eyre in the middle, The Picture of Dorian Gray rests on top. His heart is racing and he feels that something very bad is about to happen. He hears the laughter of a small child and, noticing for the first time there is a gap in the wood panelling, he sees a flash of white behind it. He peers behind the open panel and views a flight of wooden stairs beyond, leading upwards. It is a secret entrance to a passageway that he never knew existed. He hears more laughter and is compelled to further investigate the staircase.

"Alfred, come and find me!" the voice calls to him. He cannot stop himself and he makes his way up the tight spiral staircase, squeezing his bulk through the narrowing spaces. "Who is there?" he shouts, but more laughter is the only sound he hears. Twisting and winding further and higher, it is totally dark now. He starts to feel a pain in his chest and knows he is a fool for not abandoning this venture. At least when he reaches the top there will be cool air on the roof, he thinks, and he would have trouble turning around in the restricted space in order to go back down. Whatever has he got himself into, he wonders. Now he can see a square of light as he nears the top. He pulls himself through the hatch and is thankful to gasp some deep breaths of cool air. He checks around himself and the roof space; there is no one there, no laughter to be heard now. He makes his way to the edge of the roof with only a slight gradient, and takes in the view of the lush greenery of the estate. It is lucky that he doesn't know it, but it's the last sight he will ever see, apart from a blur of grey bricks and a flash of black ravens as suddenly he is shoved from behind. The roof slates slide away beneath his feet. Time elapses in slow motion as he free falls to the ground, hitting it with a sickening thud, lying twisted and smashed, his neck snapped and spinal cord severed.

"Goodbye, Alfred, good riddance!" calls Briar from the shadows, as if waving him off on his terminal trip.

Chapter 19

In the seventeenth century the site which was then known as Corvid's Plantation housed a small hamlet on top of the hill. This was a well situated place to live as it could not be flooded or be subject to mudslides, a fate which befell the villages that occupied the lower ground.

Hetha Hedgeley was a notable figure in the area due to her fortune telling abilities which were encouraged by some and shunned by others. She attracted an air of suspicion as some were frightened of her possible supernatural abilities, which they neither welcomed or understood. More of her prophecies came true than those which did not and this led to her being avoided, based on a fear that she was bewitched. Her striking appearance set her apart from others. Her flame-red hair was an unusual feature but the fact she had heterochromia iridum, one green eye and one brown eye, made her even more remarkable and curious. She gained a reputation for being the *village shamen*. It was rumoured that she could cast spells, though not necessarily with the intention to cause harm. This lack of understanding and fear of being 'hexed' caused her to be generally shunned and only sought out by those who wanted her help. Such wariness helped to consolidate beliefs that Hetha was not one to be trusted.

Scaremongering stories were circulated; tales of dead animals being resurrected by her on an altar in the woods or that she was able to contact spirits and perform acts of sorcery. It was true that she understood herbalism and how to cure ailments using the nature's produce that was locally available. She would cut a variety of twigs, leaves and berries to make healing infusions. If someone was ill and in need, they would happily take something from her that may have the power to heal. This ability helped to generate her main source of income.

When Hetha became pregnant she hid herself away as much as she could. She was not wrong when she imagined that the gossips were saying vile and malicious things, rumours of illegitimacy that she did not wish to hear. In the absence of a husband there was little she could do to defend herself against such claims.

In the autumn she gave birth to twin girls who looked exactly like her, and exactly like each other. The esoteric trio were stared at from afar and avoided close-up. She named the girls Hester and Cora, and as they grew up they imitated each other's actions and invented a private language at the exclusion of others. They seldom engaged in conversation with anyone else except their mother with whom they exchanged regular words and speech. They made friends with the crows and ravens by feeding them and were enchanted that the highly intelligent birds could talk to them. Soon they were able to perform tricks and the girls formed a bond that they could never replicate with humans. To their delight the ravens started to bring them gifts such as buttons, broken jewellery and smooth stones that they found in the woods, almost every day.

The girls played together, and under the influence of Hetha made pretend potions and fashioned bizarre doll type figures from wax and clay. Sometimes they experimented with fortune telling techniques. One such divination practice known as oomancey involved the creation of a venus glass, where egg white poured into water produces images to foretell the future. For example, if the shape of a bell was formed, this could indicate a wedding, or a coffin shape might warn of impending death. Hetha had every confidence in this as she used the method to gain knowledge of her pregnancy. She rubbed an uncooked chicken egg on her belly then cracked it on a plate. The egg she selected had two yolks so she took this as a sign that she would have twins.

One day the girls saw something in the venus glass which made them totally hysterical, an omen suggesting that no good would come to them and they would one day be murdered. Soon after the revelation they began screaming out in pain, making rapid jerking movements and grimacing. Their eyes blinked excessively and then the movements changed into slow writhing. This was unfortunately witnessed by some shocked onlookers who concluded that the girls, and most likely Hetha, must be possessed by the devil.

When a peddler arrived in the village to sell his fabrics, boot laces and trinkets he tried to persuade the girls to buy something from him. They would not speak to him but nevertheless wanted to touch some of the items he was selling. He thought they were trying to steal from him and shouted angrily at them. They shouted back at him in their special language which frightened him away. When he became ill that evening the peddler blamed the girls, believing they had put a spell on him. Word began to spread to the surrounding villages that Corvid's Plantation had witches in its midst. Others in the vicinity became unwell with fever and painful swellings, and although it was not widely known, people in the villages where the peddler had previously visited were also symptomatic. Infested fleas in the cloth he carried with him from London were the infective source, yet Hester and Cora were blamed for putting a curse on him. As more and more infected cases manifested themselves in the area there was growing fear and unrest that sparked the witch hunt.

Chapter 20

In 1562 An Act Against Conjurations, Enchantments and Witchcrafts demanded the death penalty for any person who exercised such acts which had caused harm to, or killed another. Anyone found guilty of such a felony would be put to death using a variety of horrific means.

A self-appointed lawyer became The Witch-finder General, paid to hunt out a person or group of people whose views were considered unorthodox, or who were a threat to society. The allegations were taken seriously and the Hedgeleys were wanted for engaging in occult acts with the devil. Together with a mob of female assistants The General made his way to Covid's Plantation to capture and question them. There was little time to understand what was happening, or indeed, to get away. They tried to escape the clutches of the mob by running into the woods to save themselves, but were outnumbered, grabbed roughly and put in shackles. The assistants carried out examinations to look for devil's marks and determined that flea bites on their wrists and ankles, their generalised peculiar appearance and non-matching eye colours were precisely the signs they were looking for. Despite the Hedgeleys' vocal protests, kicking and biting, they were loaded onto a cart which would transport them to prison. It was a humiliating journey for they were jeered at and goaded all along the route. Some threw sticks, stones and rotten fruit at the passing cart. At the journey's end they were left to languish in a pitch-black dungeon in deplorable conditions whilst awaiting trial. Nothing would stand in the way of the witch cleansing programme and the mob received their payment for the successful apprehension and incarceration. Nothing the Hedgeleys could say or do would convince the court that they were anything other than guilty. Their fate was already sealed.

Then came the shocking finale, the day where they were taken to a deep lake for *ordeal by water.* They refused to confess and protested their innocence to the very end. A rope was tied around their waists. Hester and Cora's thumbs were tied to their opposing great toes and they were flung in the water. It was ultimately the most unfair test to determine their witch status. If they floated, they were supported by invisible demons and therefore guilty, and if they sank, they would be declared innocent. Hetha watched her girls drown together, and if that was not her worst punishment, she was then taken to the top of Corvid's Plantation hill. There she joined the other 'witches' who had been taken there to share the barbaric fate of being burned at the stake.

Chapter 21

Rookery Heights should never have been built here. It is easy to say that now, given the history of misfortune that has interwoven through its fabric over the last couple of centuries.

Alfred's death left the household in a state of great sadness and shock once more and Lord Charlesworth felt the pain of his friend's death the most acutely of all. He could not understand the circumstances of how or why Alfred came to be on the roof. Who had lit the fire? He considered that Alfred may have had a heart attack before he fell, but at the current time there were no answers. Maybe they would never find out what happened. Although he has thought it many times before, he is now more certain than ever, that they cannot remain at Rookery Heights. He looks back at his sister's death from tuberculosis, the sudden and unexplained death of his brother. It is too much to bear. Without discussing it openly he began to make plans. He would find somewhere else for them to live, a place of safety for their servants and especially Beatrice and their unborn child, before it's too late.

Rookery Heights is filled with negative energy, a miasma that envelops the place, poisoning and polluting the existence of its inhabitants. Lord Charlesworth cannot take any more risks. He must face the fact that his home is a liminal place between the worlds of the living and the dead, where vengeful spirits roam. They restlessly seek to have their grievances addressed for having died in despair, or having suffered an early death they cannot reconcile. Their spirits are lingering around in a no man's land instead of crossing over into the dimension of eternal light and peace. The misdemeanours that happened in the past are enshrined here, they cannot be forgiven and all of the lost, misguided spirits are attracted there, bringing about misery, havoc and death. Father O'Leary refused to carry out an exorcism as he felt that the evil forces would be too powerful and dangerous for him to singularly take on.

Everything in the house is getting packed up in readiness for a move to downsized premises in London. Lady Charlesworth is looking forward to a new start and all of the servants wish to stay with the family except Emma. She has lately been walking out with Jack and is soon to become Mrs Fortesque-Merritt. Jack is determined to finish all of the work assignments but he will not work at Rookery Heights any longer, after the ghostly encounters he experienced. The thought of being watched by a malevolent ghost and possibly being harmed is out of the question, and he is impatient to remove Emma to safety.

The house move is all arranged but just before it comes to fruition, something surprising happens to change the plans. An official letter arrives for Lord Charlesworth from Messrs. Pinkerton and Ellis, Solicitors to Mr Alfred Fallowfield (deceased). The content relates to his Last Will and Testament confirming that he has bequeathed his Crosby Hall home to Lord and Lady Charlesworth. Enclosed with the papers is a personal letter from Alfred to them, outlining his final wishes and giving thanks for their support and friendship. In the absence of any close family members who he wished to benefit from his legacy, this was his decision. He hoped they would live happily and in safety herein at Crosby Hall.

So the move was effected as quickly as possible and a new chapter began. Bessie would replace Emma and take on her new role as housemaid. Lady Charlesworth gave birth to a healthy boy who they named Edgar Alfred. He brought them all joy, healing and a reason to celebrate a new chapter in their lives.

Rookery Heights was put up for sale and although it was bare of furniture and possessions, it was not empty, and never would be, as not all of its inhabitants had vacated.

FOR SALE :
Rookery Heights. Large, historic manor house on private estate.
An excellent opportunity to purchase a spacious family home has newly presented itself. Situated on top of a hill with stunning views of the surrounding countryside, the estate features a maze, a folly and lakes. The grand entrance hall has a sweeping staircase leading to eight bedrooms (including a nursery) and three bathrooms. The property has a pleasant drawing room and parlour which is perfect for entertaining guests. A comfortable library is accommodated on the upper floor. Servant quarters are housed below stairs where a large, well equipped kitchen with pantry is situated. A walled courtyard encloses a selection of out-houses and stables. Potential buyers should promptly apply to our agent for disclosure of further details and sale price as this unique property is certain to generate much interest.

~~~~~~oOo~~~~~~

Credits

The wordage of the sign that hung above the servant quarters at Rookery Heights was taken from a real-life quotation found at the residence of the York family, Erddig Hall, North Wales. The author is unknown.

Printed in Great Britain
by Amazon